6

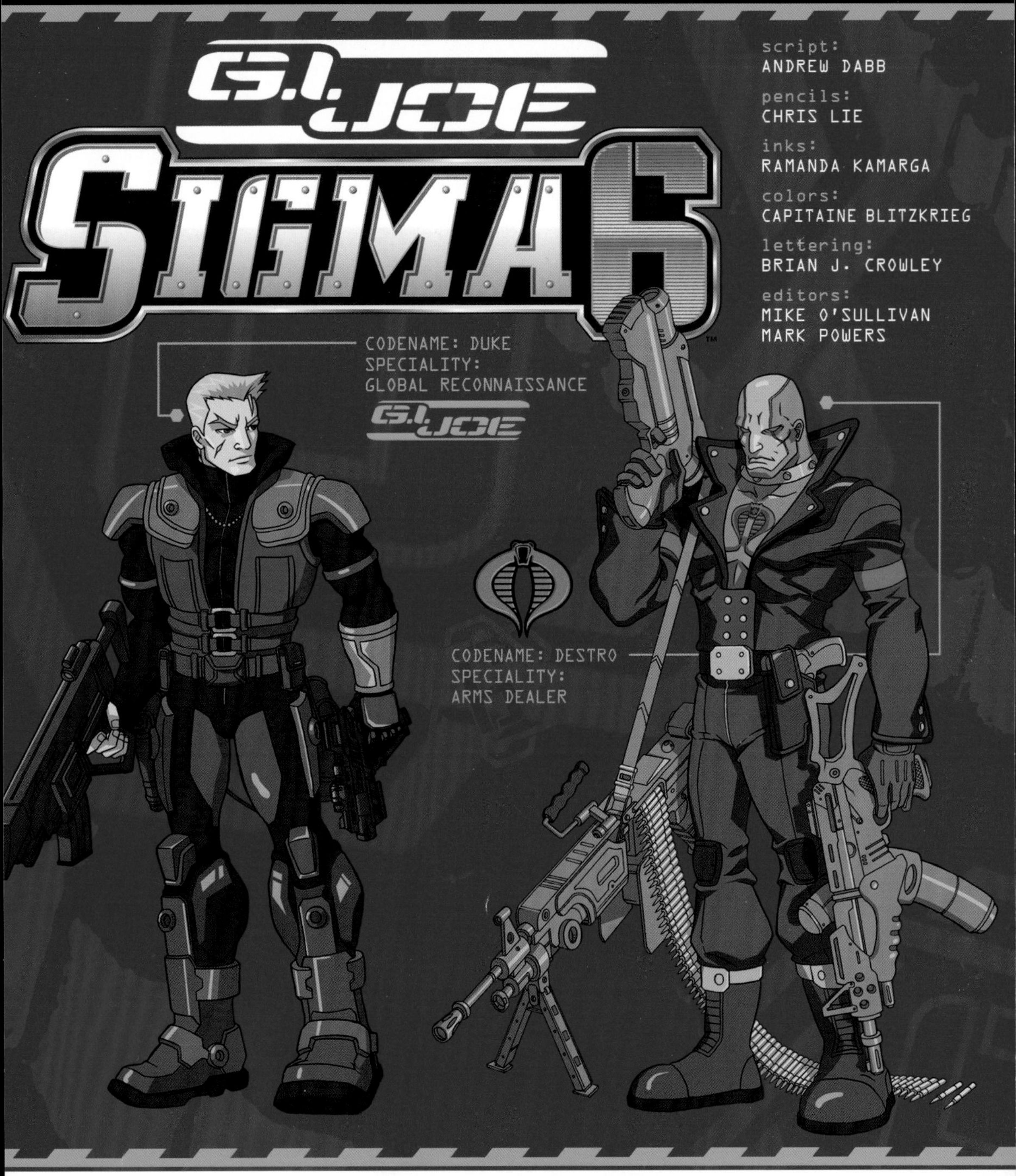
G.I. JOE
SIGMA 6
script:
ANDREW DABB
pencils:
CHRIS LIE
inks:
RAMANDA KAMARGA
colors:
CAPITAINE BLITZKRIEG
lettering:
BRIAN J. CROWLEY
editors:
MIKE O'SULLIVAN
MARK POWERS
CODENAME: DUKE
SPECIALITY:
GLOBAL RECONNAISSANCE
G.I. JOE
CODENAME: DESTRO
SPECIALITY:
ARMS DEALER

DEPTH

DDP

Spotlight

visit us at www.abdopublishing.com

Exclusive reinforced library bound edition published in 2008 by Spotlight, a division of ABDO Publishing Group, Edina, Minnesota. This edition is produced under agreement with Devils Due Publishing, Inc. www.devilsdue.net

Library of Congress Cataloging-in-Publication Data

Dabb, Andrew.

Depth / script, Andrew Dabb ; pencils, Chris Lie ; inks, Ramanda Kamarga ; colors, Grafiksismik ; lettering, Brian J. Crowley ; editors, Mike O'Sullivan, Mark Powers. -- Exclusive reinforced library bound ed.

p. cm. -- (G.I. Joe SIGMA 6)

Revision of issue 1 (Nov. 2005) of G.I. Joe SIGMA 6.

ISBN-13: 978-1-59961-370-3

ISBN-10: 1-59961-370-0

I. Lie, Chris. II. O'Sullivan, Mike. III. Powers, Mark. IV. G.I. Joe SIGMA 6. 1. V. Title.

PN6727.D23D46 2008

741.5'973--dc22

2006052224

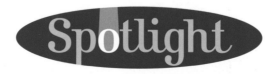

All Spotlight books have reinforced library bindings and are manufactured in the United States of America.

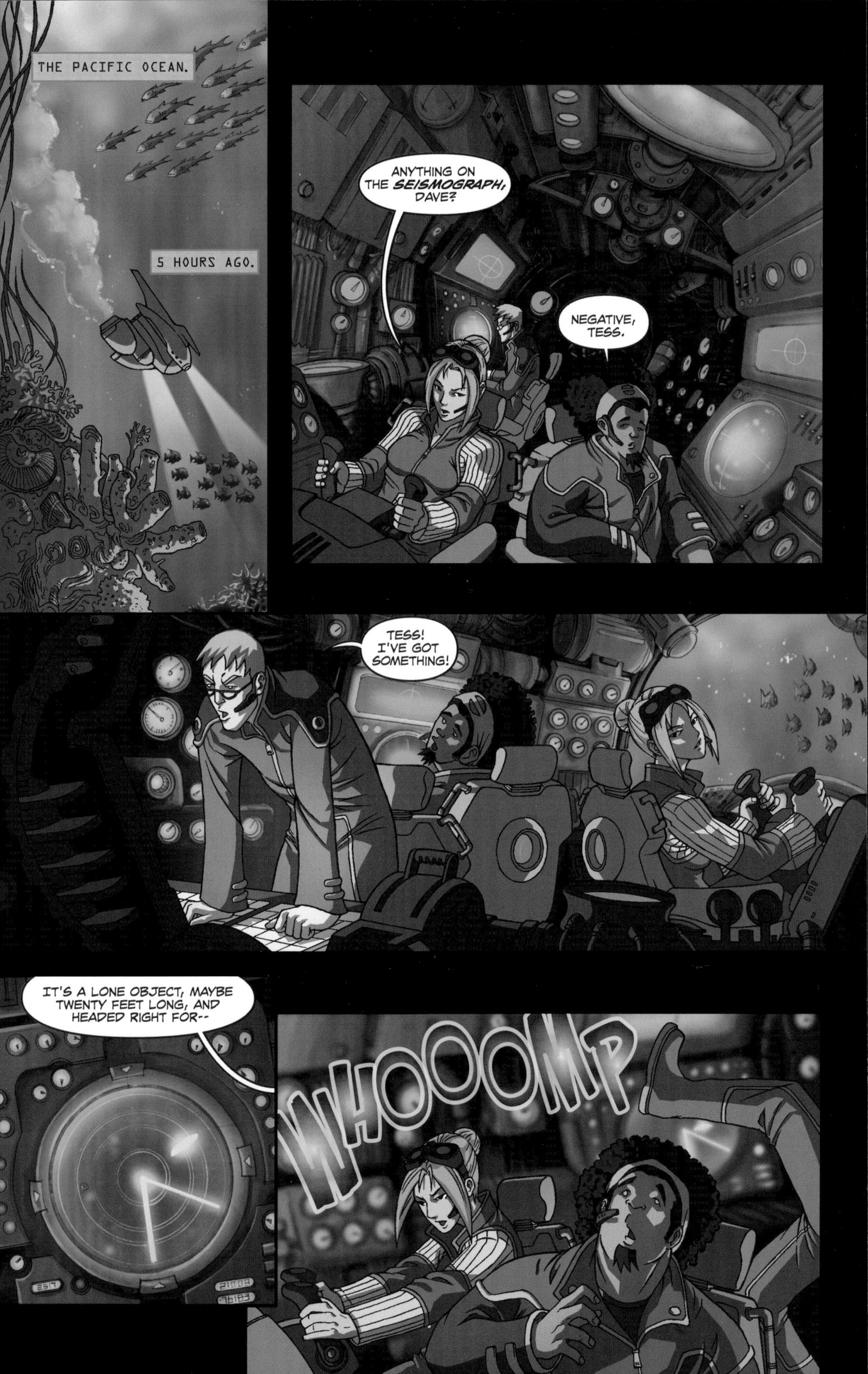
THE PACIFIC OCEAN.
5 HOURS AGO.
ANYTHING ON THE SEISMOGRAPH, DAVE?
NEGATIVE, TESS.
TESS! I'VE GOT SOMETHING!
IT'S A LONE OBJECT, MAYBE TWENTY FEET LONG, AND HEADED RIGHT FOR--
WHOOOMP

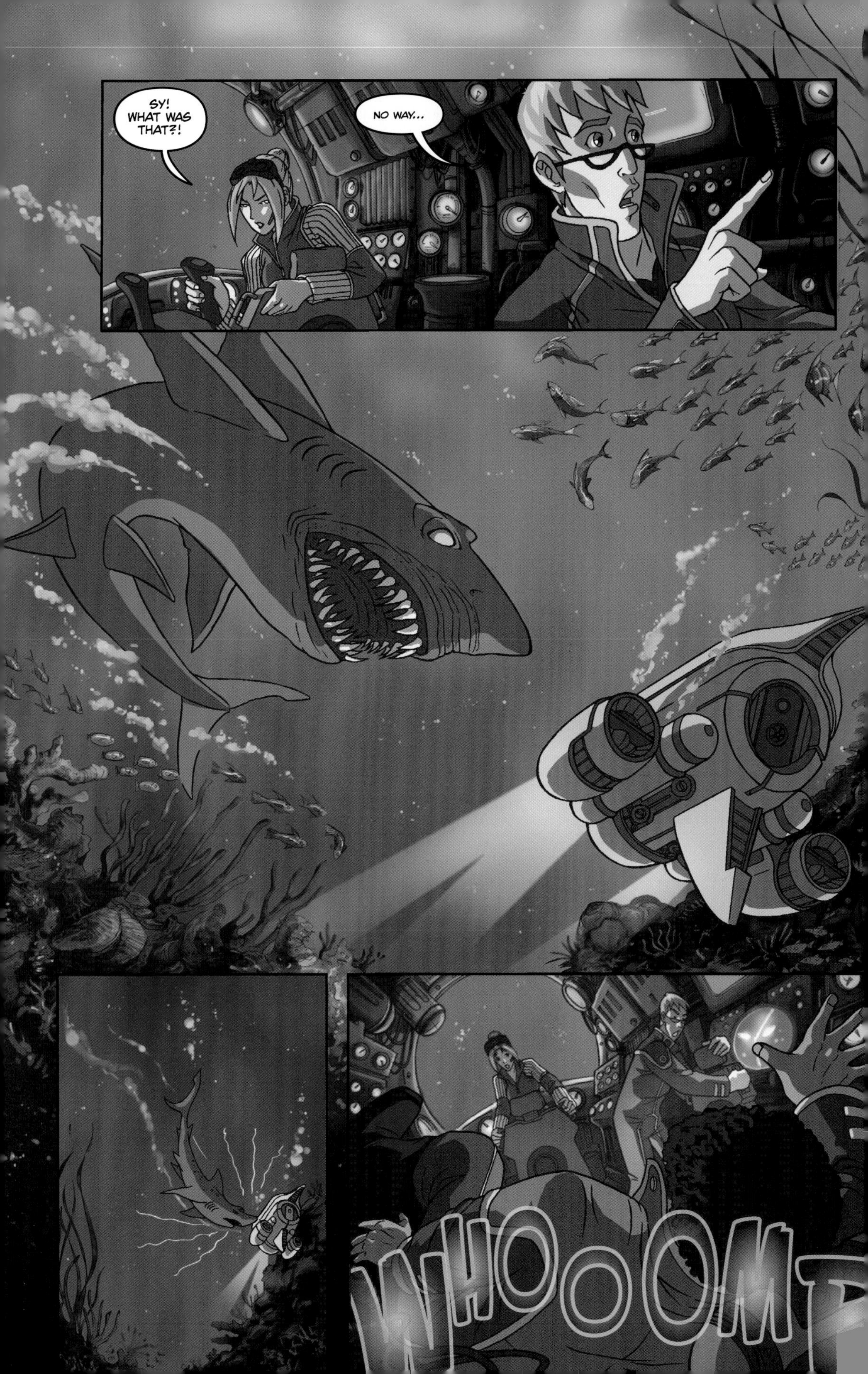
SY! WHAT WAS THAT?!
NO WAY...
WHOOOMP

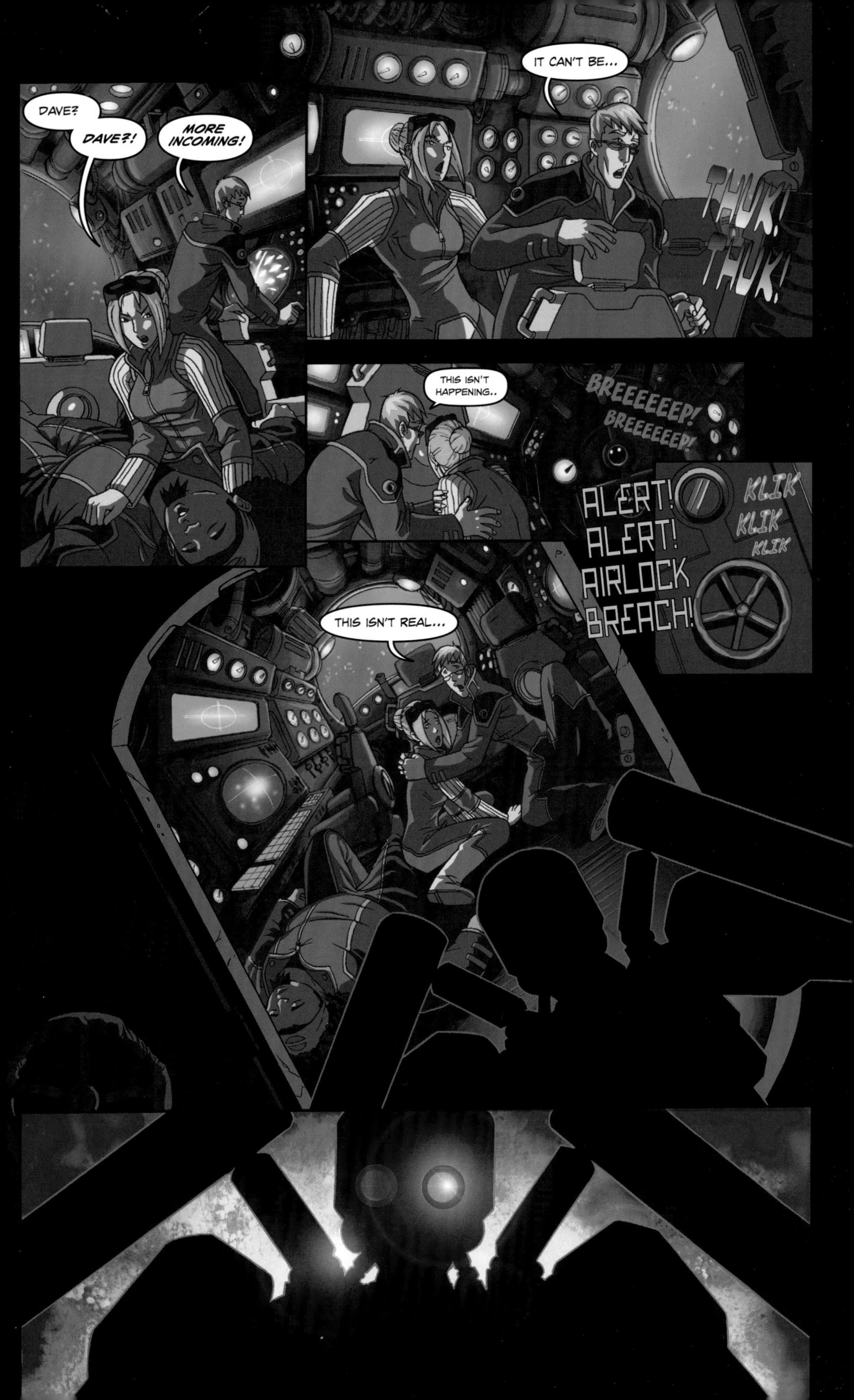

DAVE?
DAVE?!
MORE INCOMING!
IT CAN'T BE...
THUK! THUK!
THIS ISN'T HAPPENING..
BREEEEEEP! BREEEEEEP!
ALERT! ALERT! AIRLOCK BREACH!
KLIK KLIK KLIK
THIS ISN'T REAL...

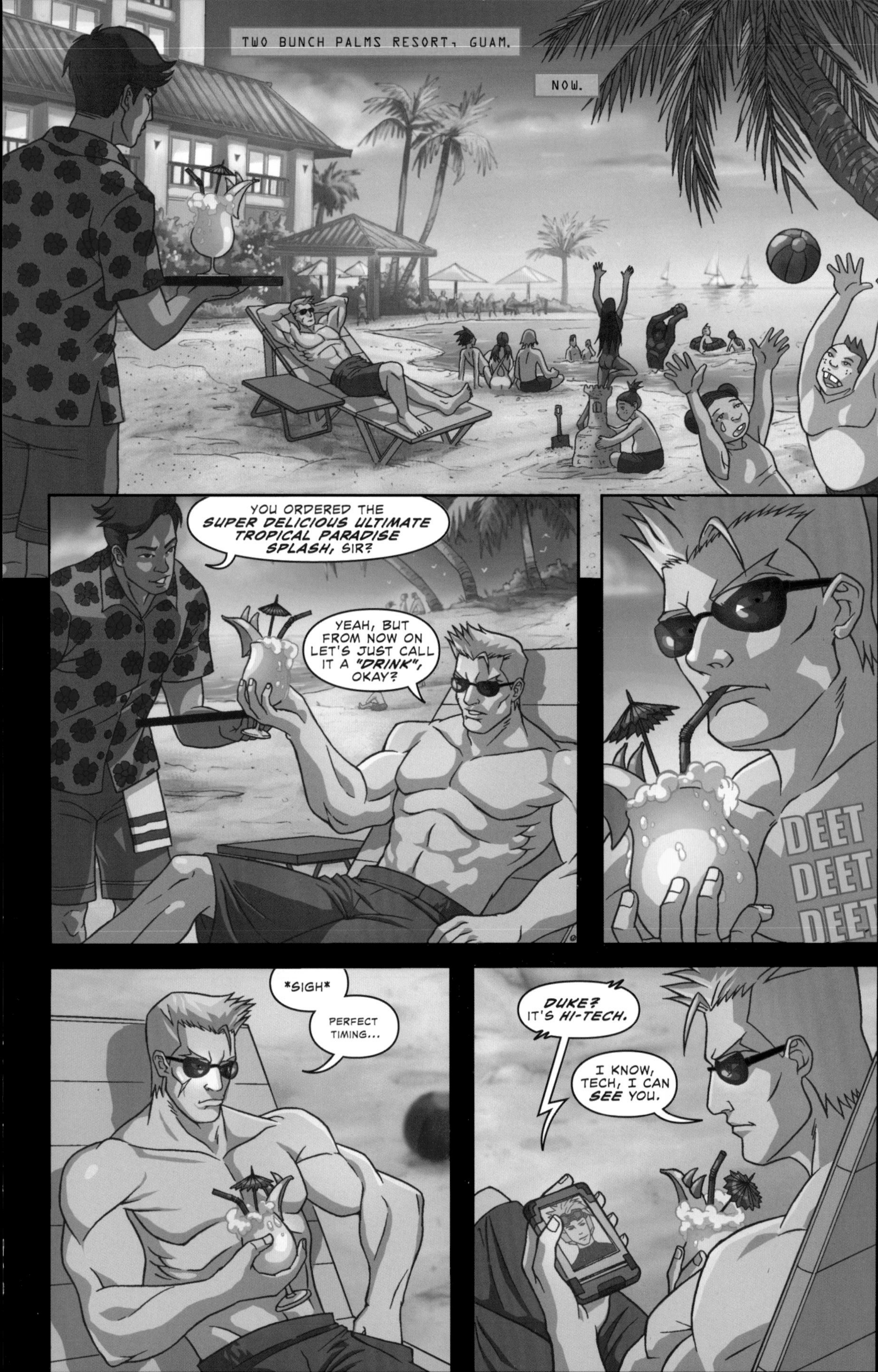
TWO BUNCH PALMS RESORT, GUAM.
NOW.
YOU ORDERED THE SUPER DELICIOUS ULTIMATE TROPICAL PARADISE SPLASH, SIR?
YEAH, BUT FROM NOW ON LET'S JUST CALL IT A "DRINK", OKAY?
DEET DEET DEET
SIGH
PERFECT TIMING...
DUKE? IT'S HI-TECH.
I KNOW, TECH, I CAN SEE YOU.

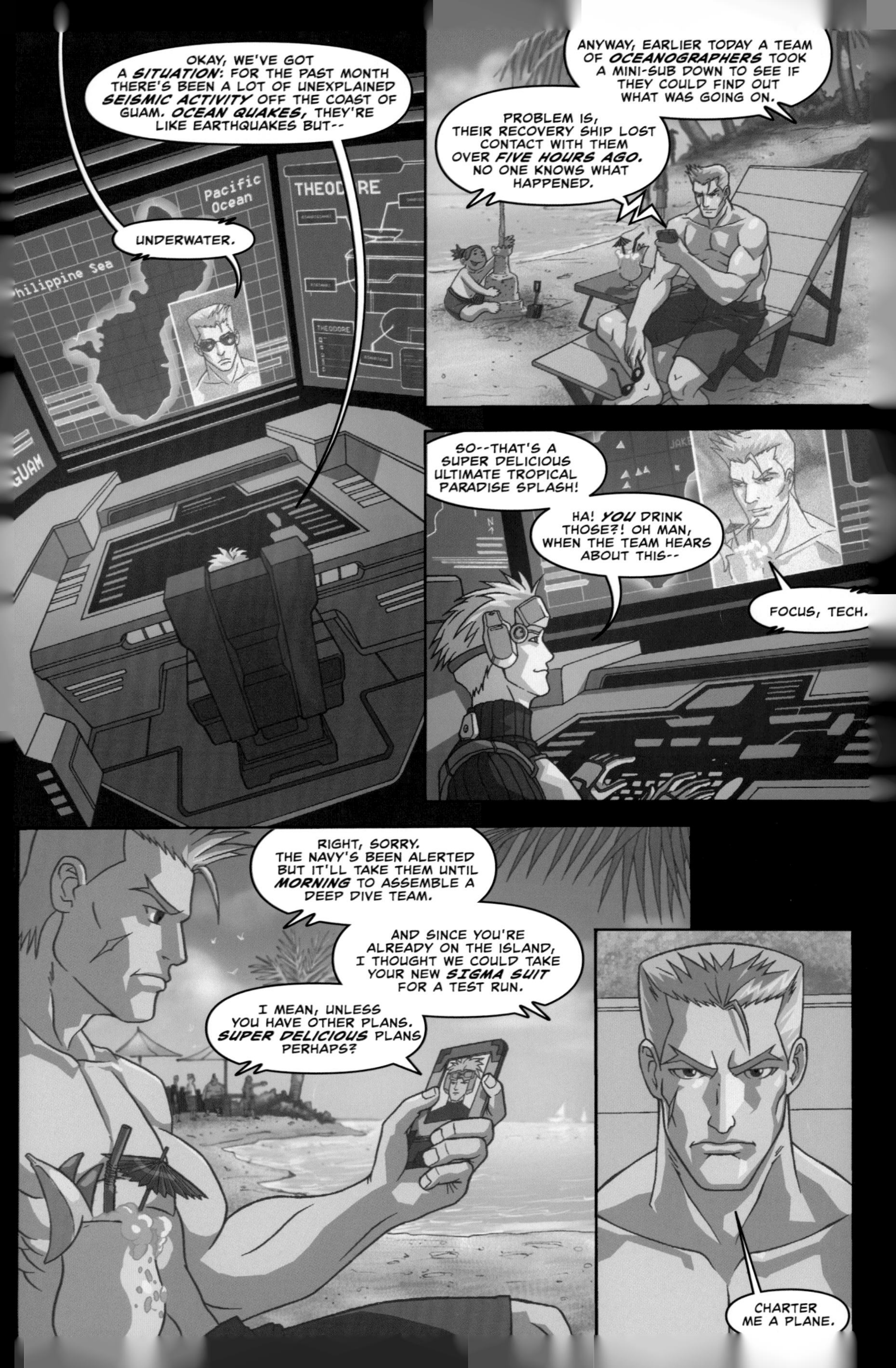

OKAY, WE'VE GOT A SITUATION: FOR THE PAST MONTH THERE'S BEEN A LOT OF UNEXPLAINED SEISMIC ACTIVITY OFF THE COAST OF GUAM. OCEAN QUAKES, THEY'RE LIKE EARTHQUAKES BUT--
UNDERWATER.
Pacific Ocean
Philippine Sea
GUAM
THEODORE
ANYWAY, EARLIER TODAY A TEAM OF OCEANOGRAPHERS TOOK A MINI-SUB DOWN TO SEE IF THEY COULD FIND OUT WHAT WAS GOING ON.
PROBLEM IS, THEIR RECOVERY SHIP LOST CONTACT WITH THEM OVER FIVE HOURS AGO. NO ONE KNOWS WHAT HAPPENED.
SO--THAT'S A SUPER DELICIOUS ULTIMATE TROPICAL PARADISE SPLASH!
HA! YOU DRINK THOSE?! OH MAN, WHEN THE TEAM HEARS ABOUT THIS--
FOCUS, TECH.
RIGHT, SORRY. THE NAVY'S BEEN ALERTED BUT IT'LL TAKE THEM UNTIL MORNING TO ASSEMBLE A DEEP DIVE TEAM.
AND SINCE YOU'RE ALREADY ON THE ISLAND, I THOUGHT WE COULD TAKE YOUR NEW SIGMA SUIT FOR A TEST RUN.
I MEAN, UNLESS YOU HAVE OTHER PLANS. SUPER DELICIOUS PLANS PERHAPS?
CHARTER ME A PLANE.

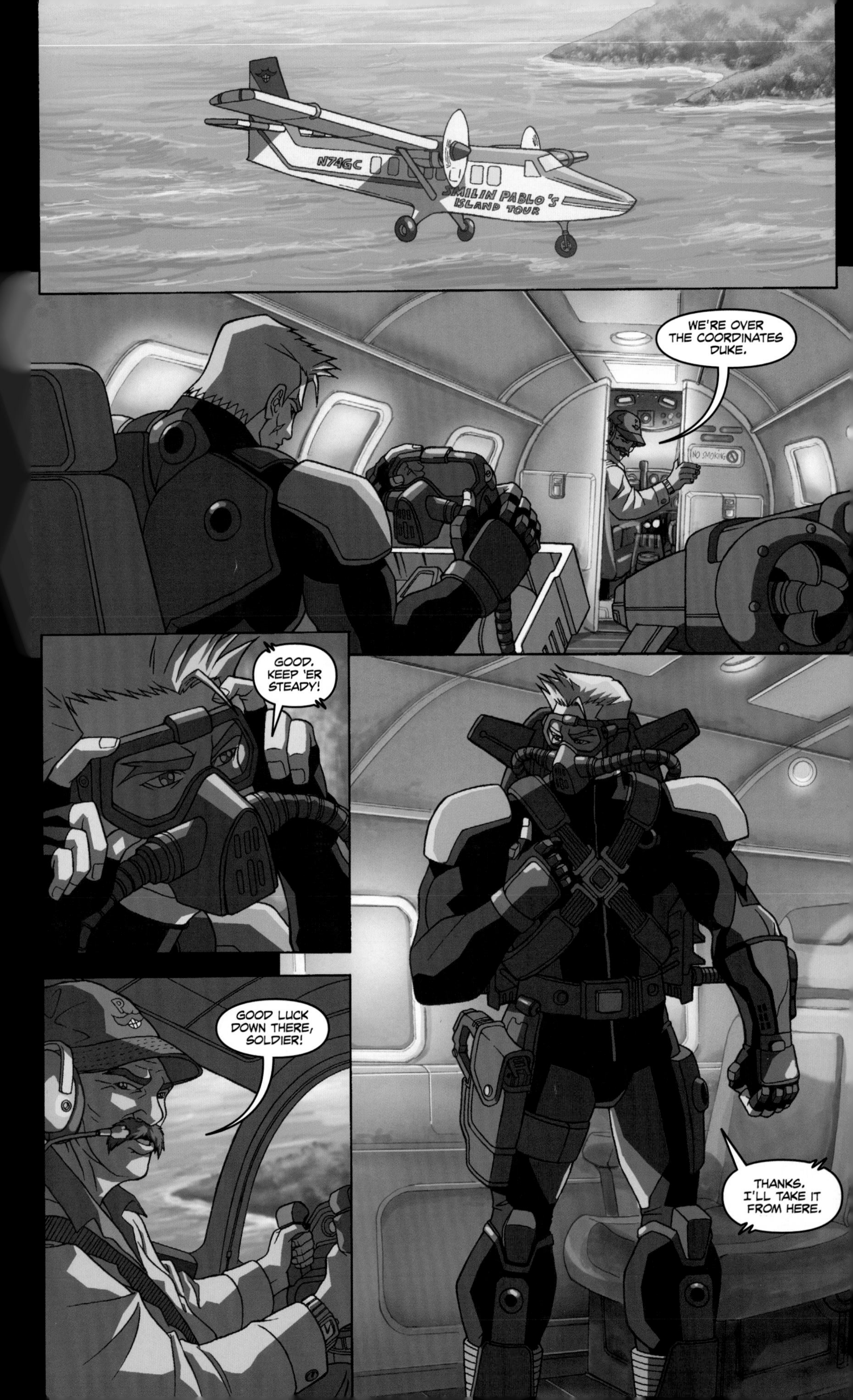
N74GC
SMILIN PABLO'S ISLAND TOUR
WE'RE OVER THE COORDINATES DUKE.
NO SMOKING
GOOD. KEEP 'ER STEADY!
GOOD LUCK DOWN THERE, SOLDIER!
THANKS. I'LL TAKE IT FROM HERE.

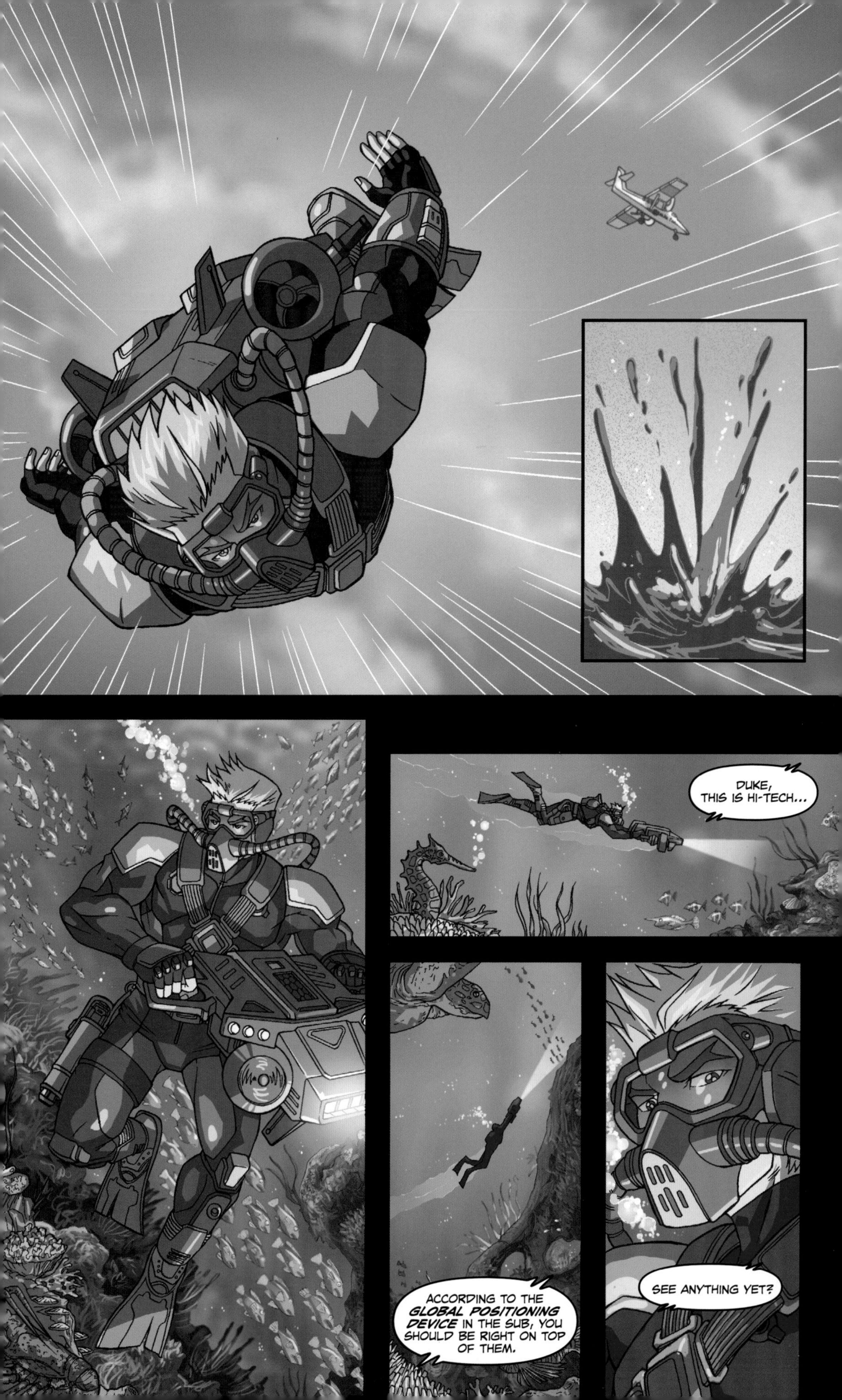
DUKE,
THIS IS HI-TECH...
ACCORDING TO THE GLOBAL POSITIONING DEVICE IN THE SUB, YOU SHOULD BE RIGHT ON TOP OF THEM.
SEE ANYTHING YET?

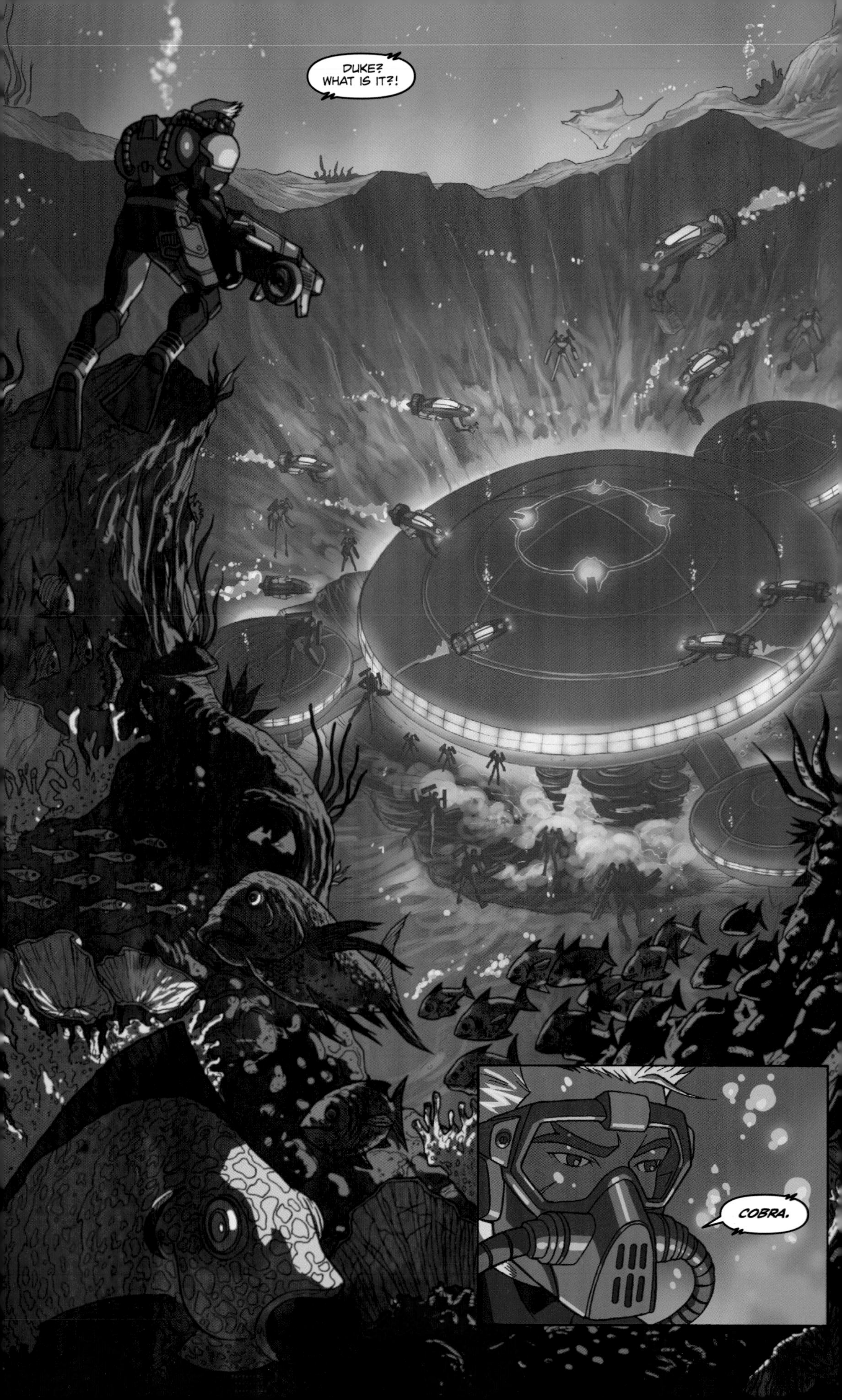
DUKE?
WHAT IS IT?!
COBRA.

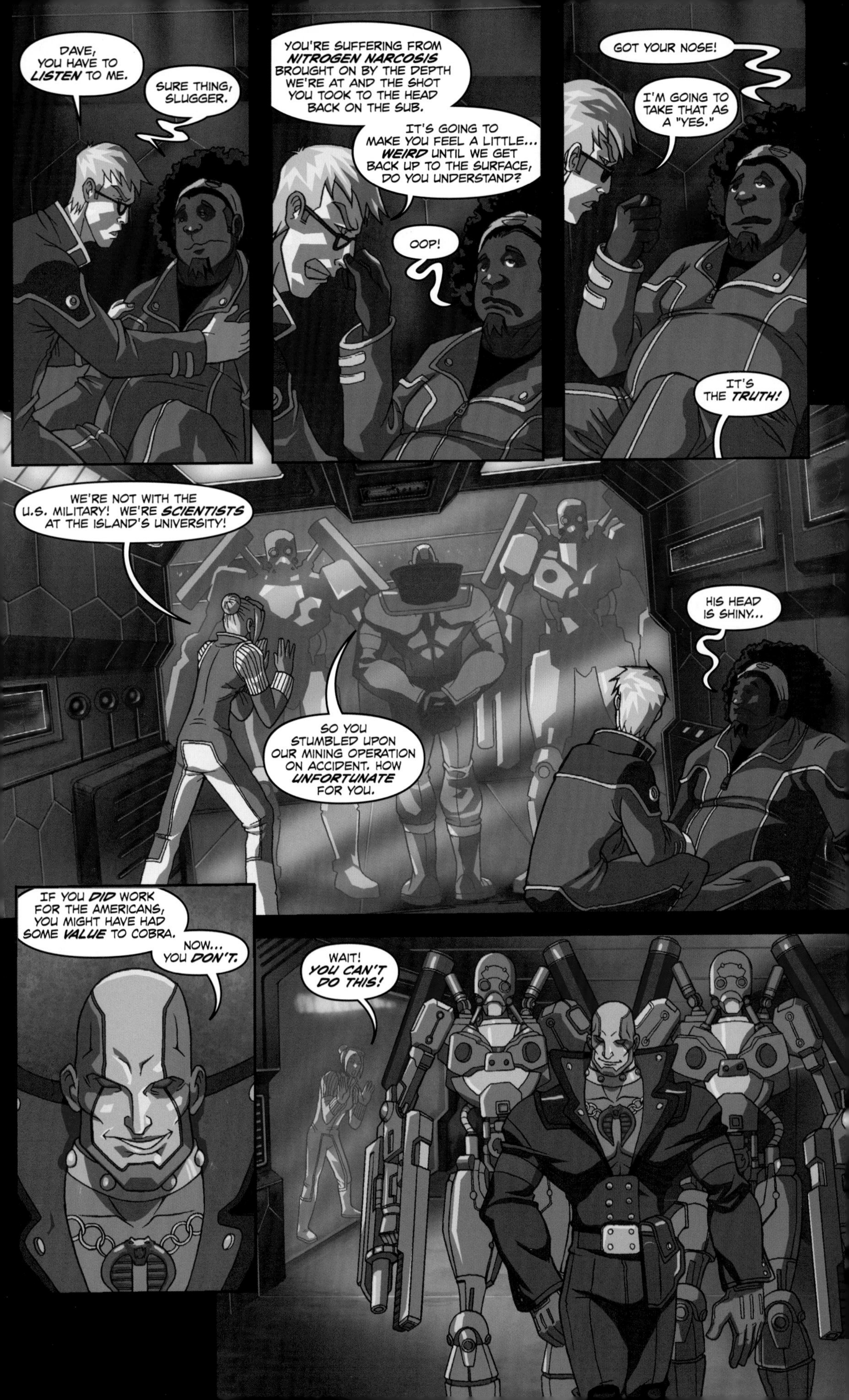
DAVE, YOU HAVE TO LISTEN TO ME.
SURE THING, SLUGGER.
YOU'RE SUFFERING FROM NITROGEN NARCOSIS BROUGHT ON BY THE DEPTH WE'RE AT AND THE SHOT YOU TOOK TO THE HEAD BACK ON THE SUB.
IT'S GOING TO MAKE YOU FEEL A LITTLE... WEIRD UNTIL WE GET BACK UP TO THE SURFACE, DO YOU UNDERSTAND?
OOP!
GOT YOUR NOSE!
I'M GOING TO TAKE THAT AS A "YES."
IT'S THE TRUTH!
WE'RE NOT WITH THE U.S. MILITARY! WE'RE SCIENTISTS AT THE ISLAND'S UNIVERSITY!
HIS HEAD IS SHINY...
SO YOU STUMBLED UPON OUR MINING OPERATION ON ACCIDENT. HOW UNFORTUNATE FOR YOU.
IF YOU DID WORK FOR THE AMERICANS, YOU MIGHT HAVE HAD SOME VALUE TO COBRA.
NOW... YOU DON'T.
WAIT! YOU CAN'T DO THIS!

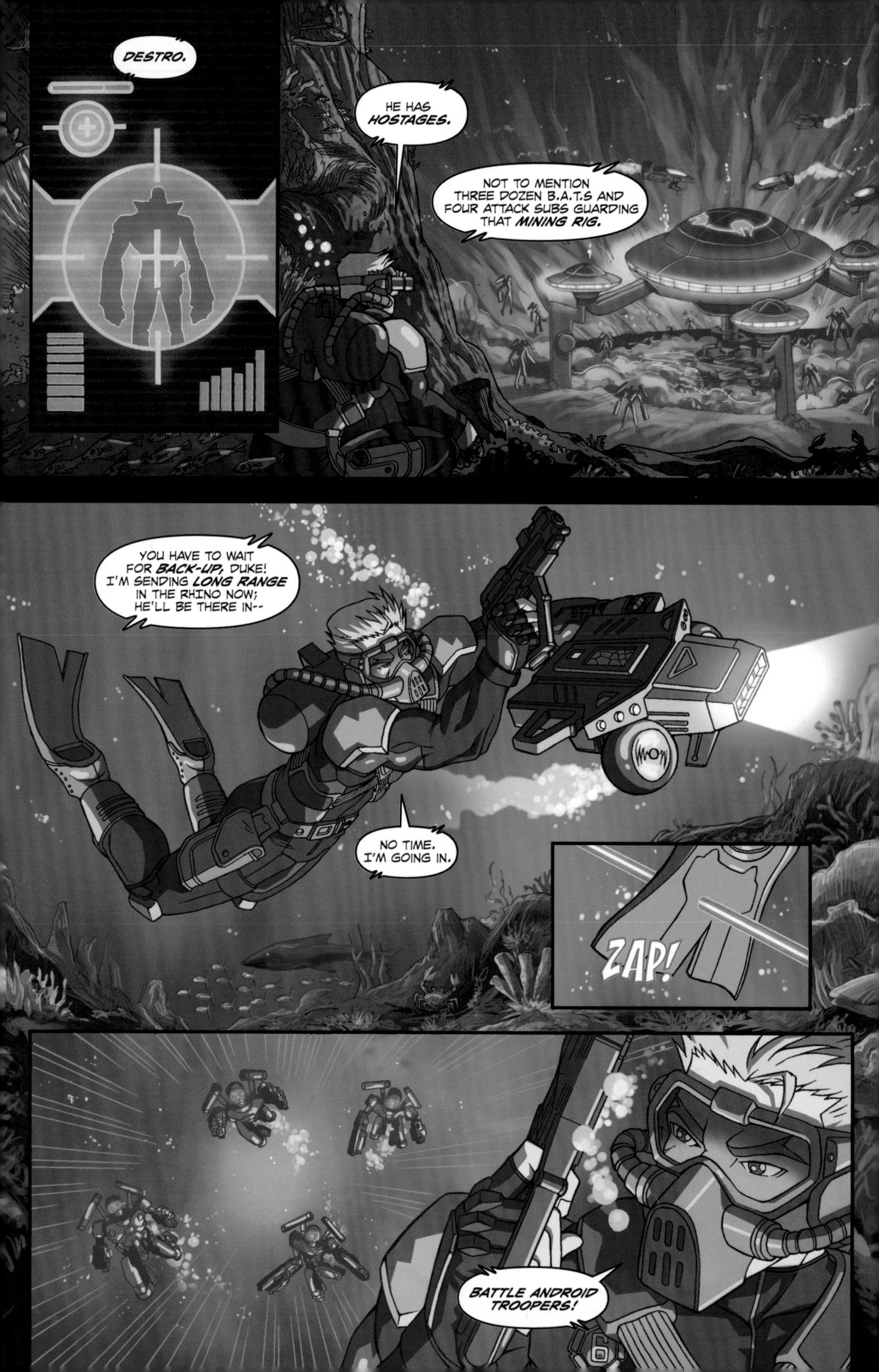
DESTRO.
HE HAS HOSTAGES.
NOT TO MENTION THREE DOZEN B.A.T.S AND FOUR ATTACK SUBS GUARDING THAT MINING RIG.
YOU HAVE TO WAIT FOR BACK-UP, DUKE! I'M SENDING LONG RANGE IN THE RHINO NOW; HE'LL BE THERE IN--
NO TIME. I'M GOING IN.
ZAP!
BATTLE ANDROID TROOPERS!

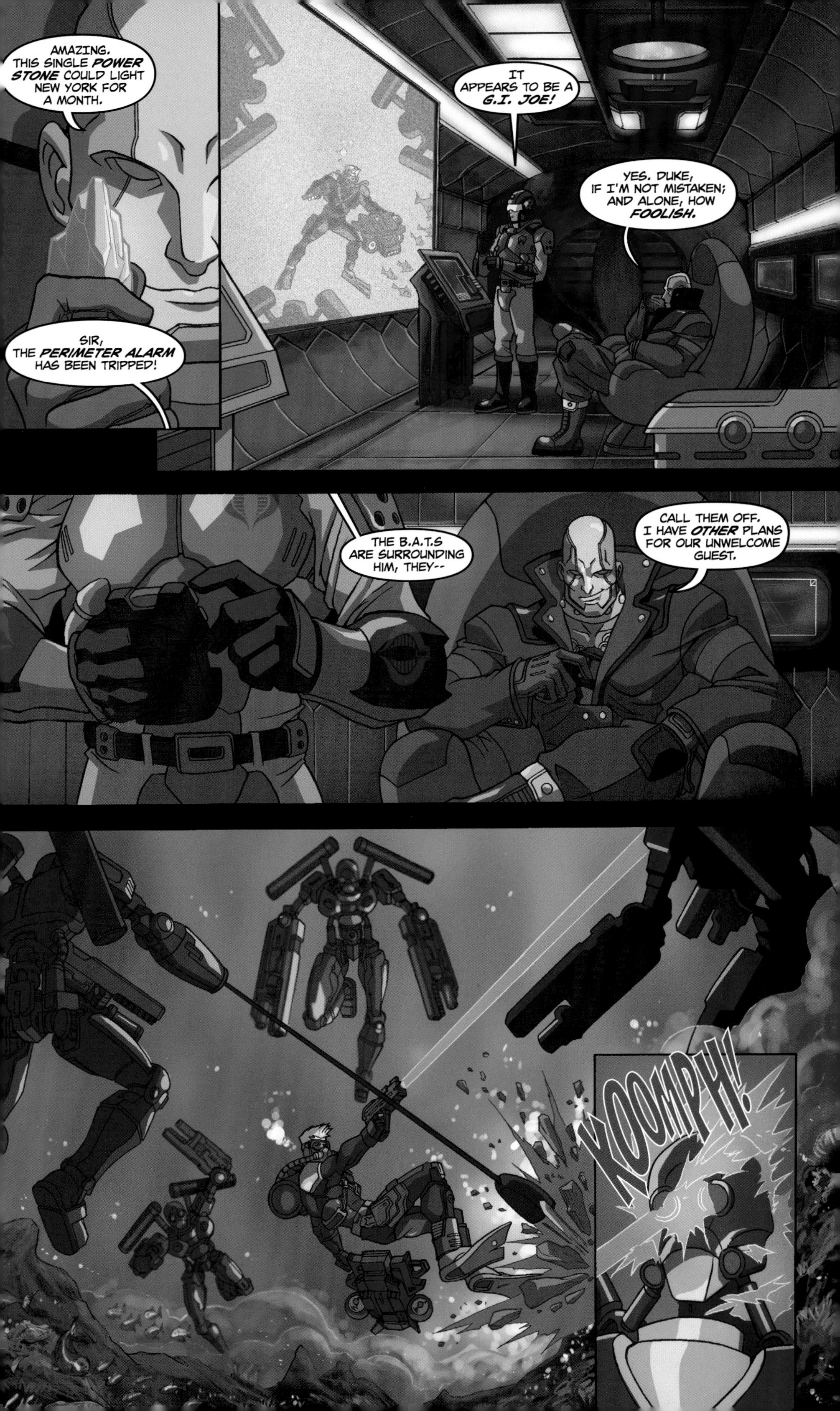
AMAZING. THIS SINGLE POWER STONE COULD LIGHT NEW YORK FOR A MONTH.
SIR, THE PERIMETER ALARM HAS BEEN TRIPPED!
IT APPEARS TO BE A G.I. JOE!
YES. DUKE, IF I'M NOT MISTAKEN; AND ALONE, HOW FOOLISH.
THE B.A.T.S ARE SURROUNDING HIM, THEY--
CALL THEM OFF. I HAVE OTHER PLANS FOR OUR UNWELCOME GUEST.
KOOMPH!

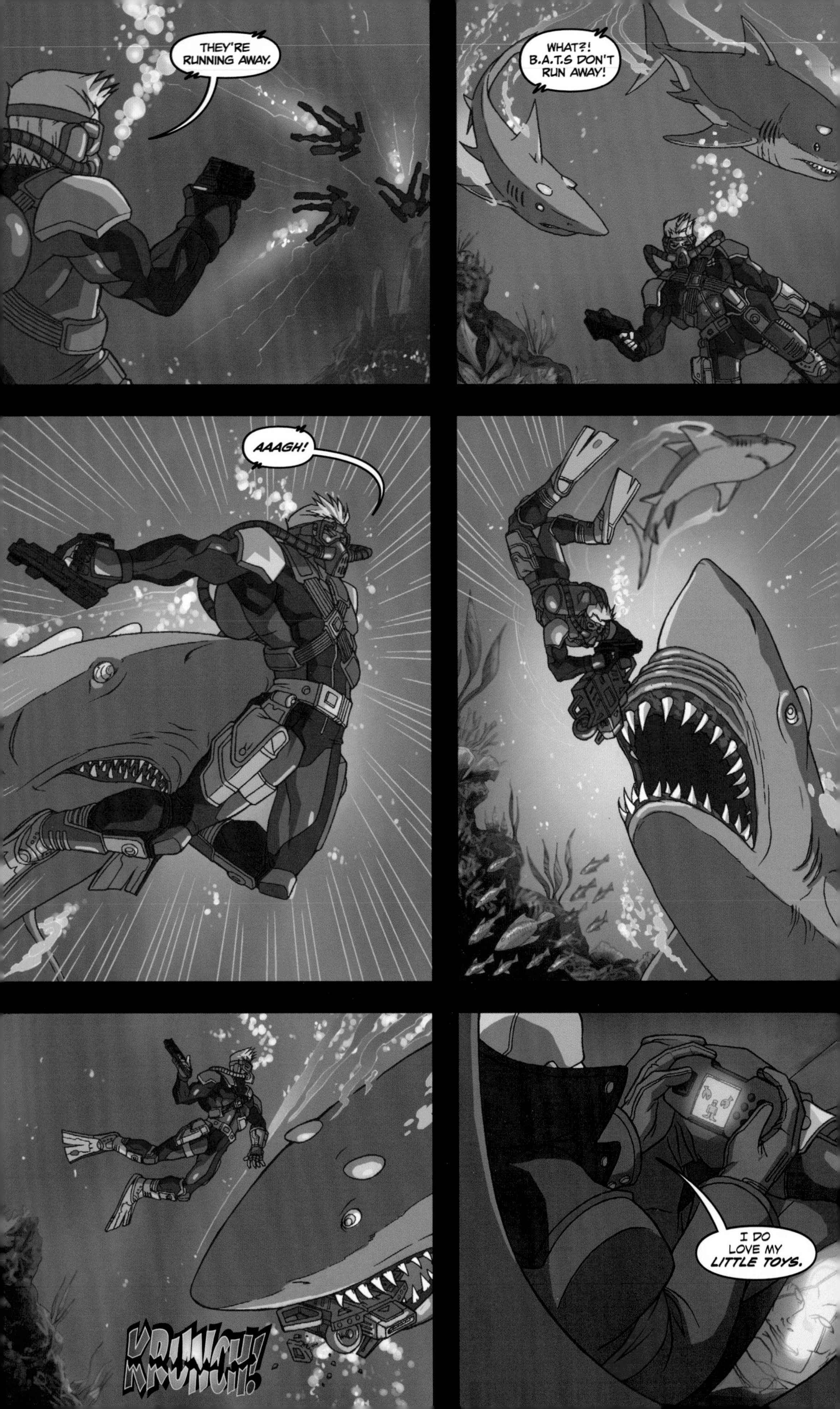
THEY'RE RUNNING AWAY.
WHAT?! B.A.T.S DON'T RUN AWAY!
AAAGH!
KRUNCH!
I DO LOVE MY LITTLE TOYS.

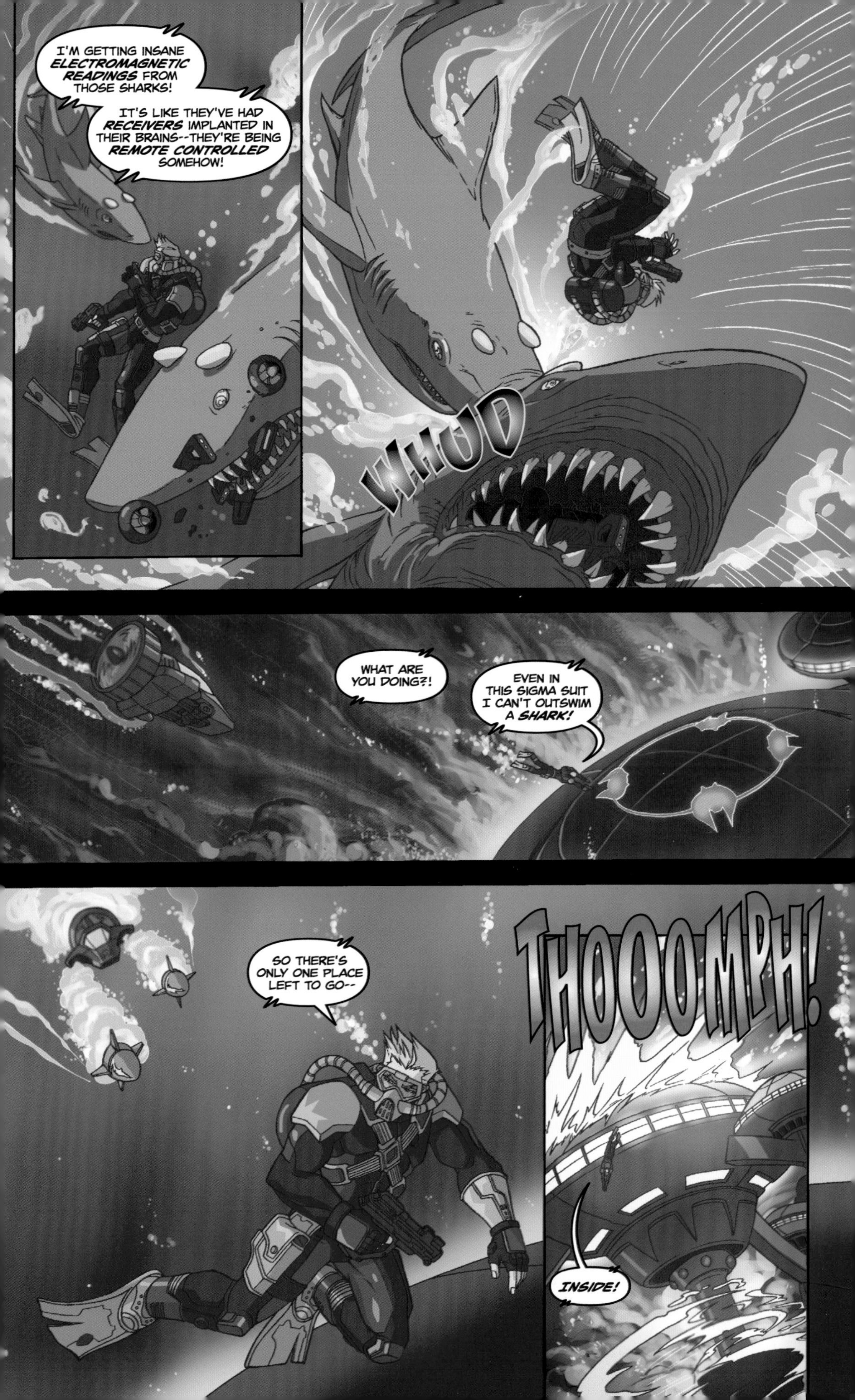
I'M GETTING INSANE ELECTROMAGNETIC READINGS FROM THOSE SHARKS!
IT'S LIKE THEY'VE HAD RECEIVERS IMPLANTED IN THEIR BRAINS--THEY'RE BEING REMOTE CONTROLLED SOMEHOW!
WHUD
WHAT ARE YOU DOING?!
EVEN IN THIS SIGMA SUIT I CAN'T OUTSWIM A SHARK!
SO THERE'S ONLY ONE PLACE LEFT TO GO--
THOOOMPH!
INSIDE!

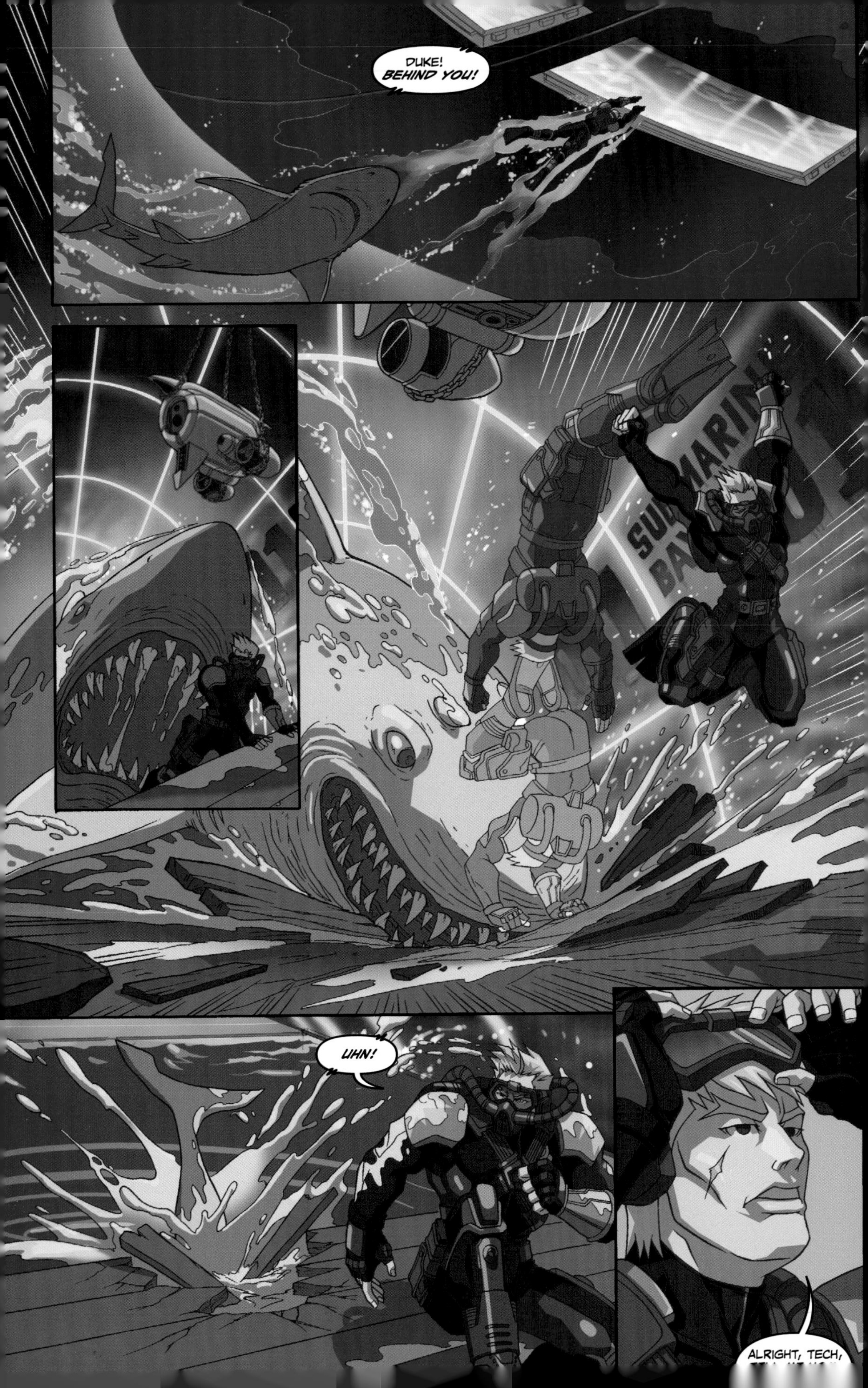
DUKE! BEHIND YOU!
UHN!
ALRIGHT, TECH,

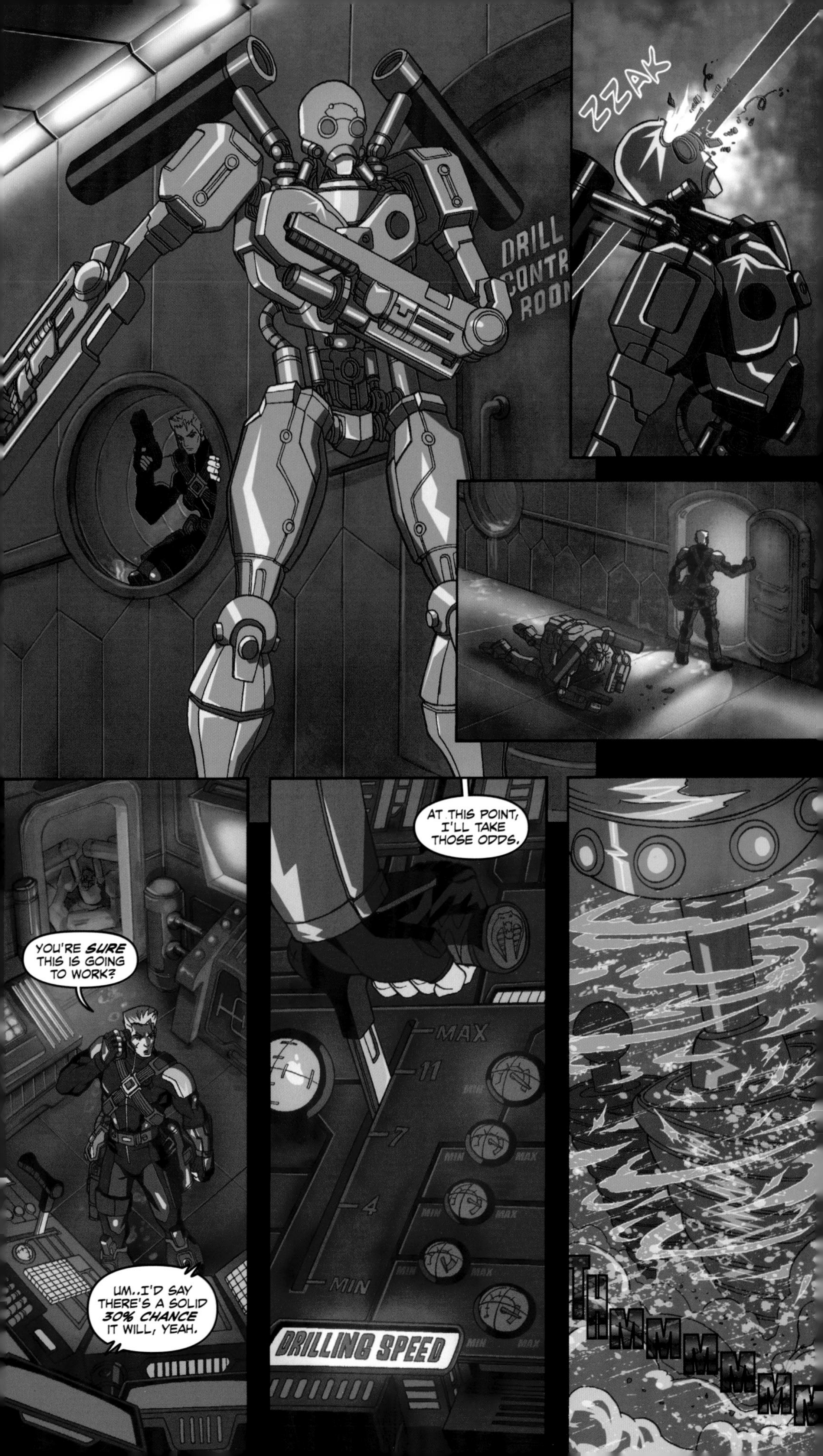
DRILL CONTR ROOM
ZZAK
YOU'RE SURE THIS IS GOING TO WORK?
UM..I'D SAY THERE'S A SOLID 30% CHANCE IT WILL, YEAH.
AT THIS POINT, I'LL TAKE THOSE ODDS.
MAX
11
7
4
MIN
DRILLING SPEED
THMMMMMMN

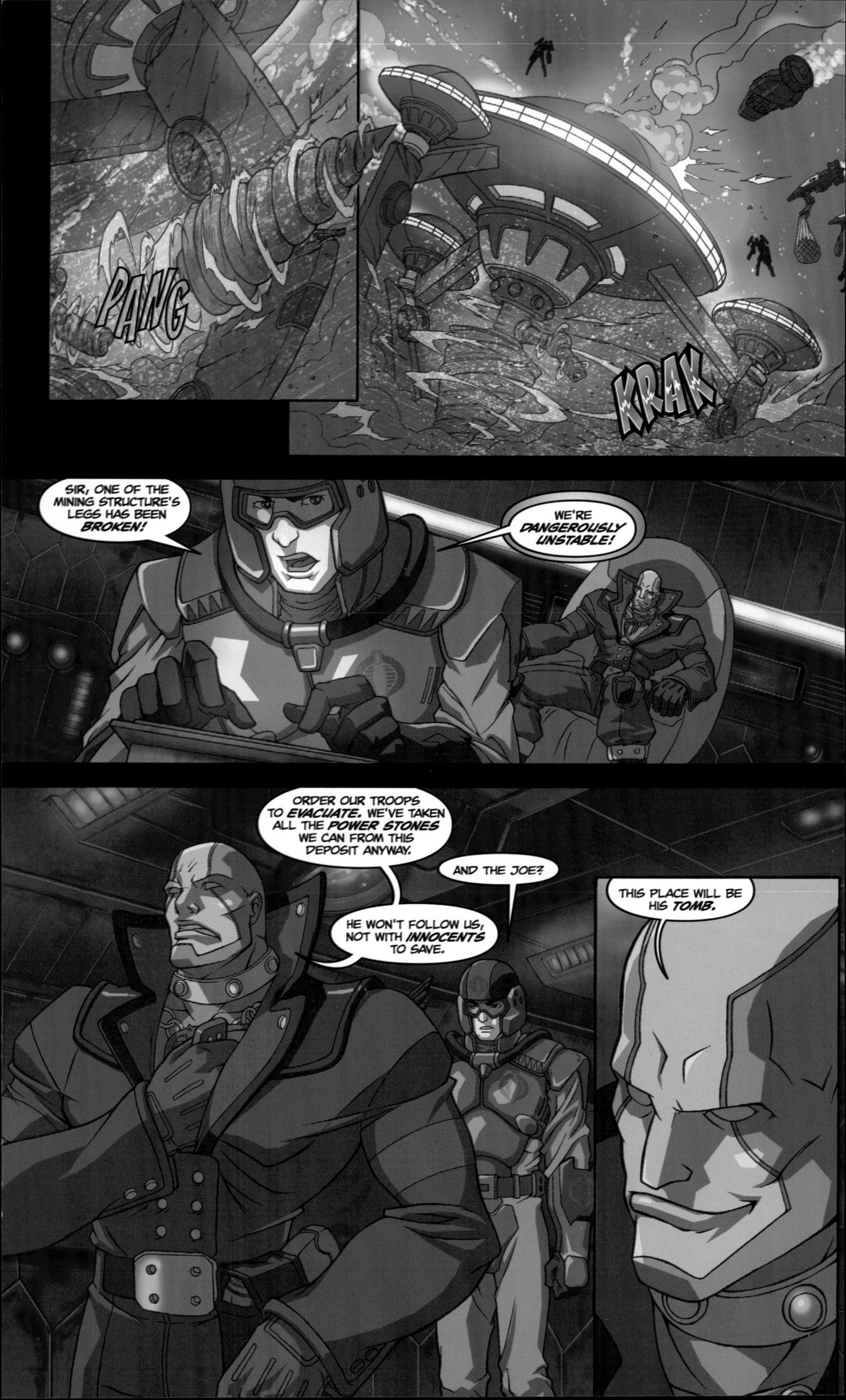
PANG
KRAK
SIR, ONE OF THE MINING STRUCTURE'S LEGS HAS BEEN BROKEN!
WE'RE DANGEROUSLY UNSTABLE!
ORDER OUR TROOPS TO EVACUATE. WE'VE TAKEN ALL THE POWER STONES WE CAN FROM THIS DEPOSIT ANYWAY.
AND THE JOE?
HE WON'T FOLLOW US, NOT WITH INNOCENTS TO SAVE.
THIS PLACE WILL BE HIS TOMB.

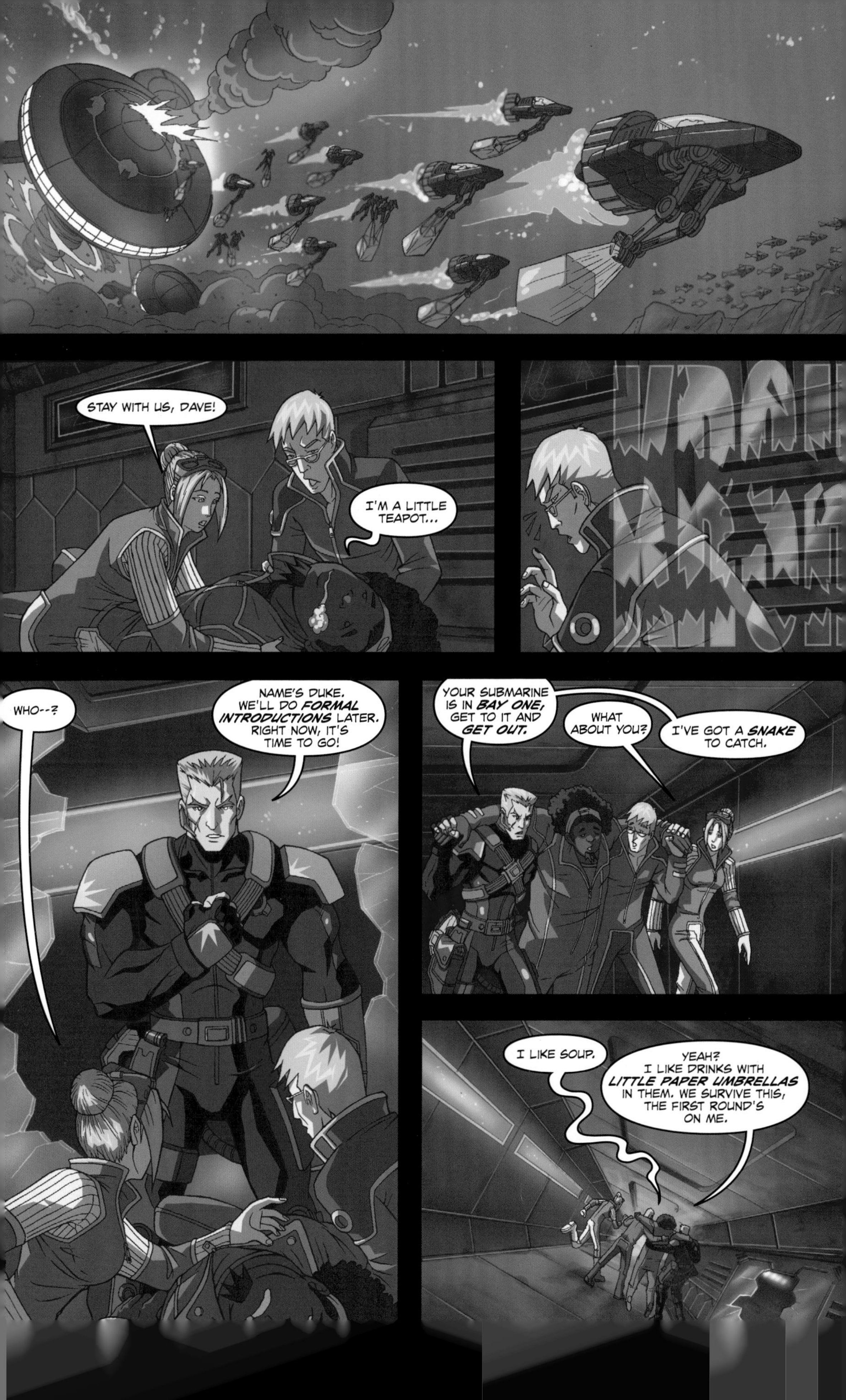
STAY WITH US, DAVE!
I'M A LITTLE TEAPOT...
WHO--?
NAME'S DUKE. WE'LL DO FORMAL INTRODUCTIONS LATER. RIGHT NOW, IT'S TIME TO GO!
YOUR SUBMARINE IS IN BAY ONE, GET TO IT AND GET OUT.
WHAT ABOUT YOU?
I'VE GOT A SNAKE TO CATCH.
I LIKE SOUP.
YEAH? I LIKE DRINKS WITH LITTLE PAPER UMBRELLAS IN THEM. WE SURVIVE THIS, THE FIRST ROUND'S ON ME.

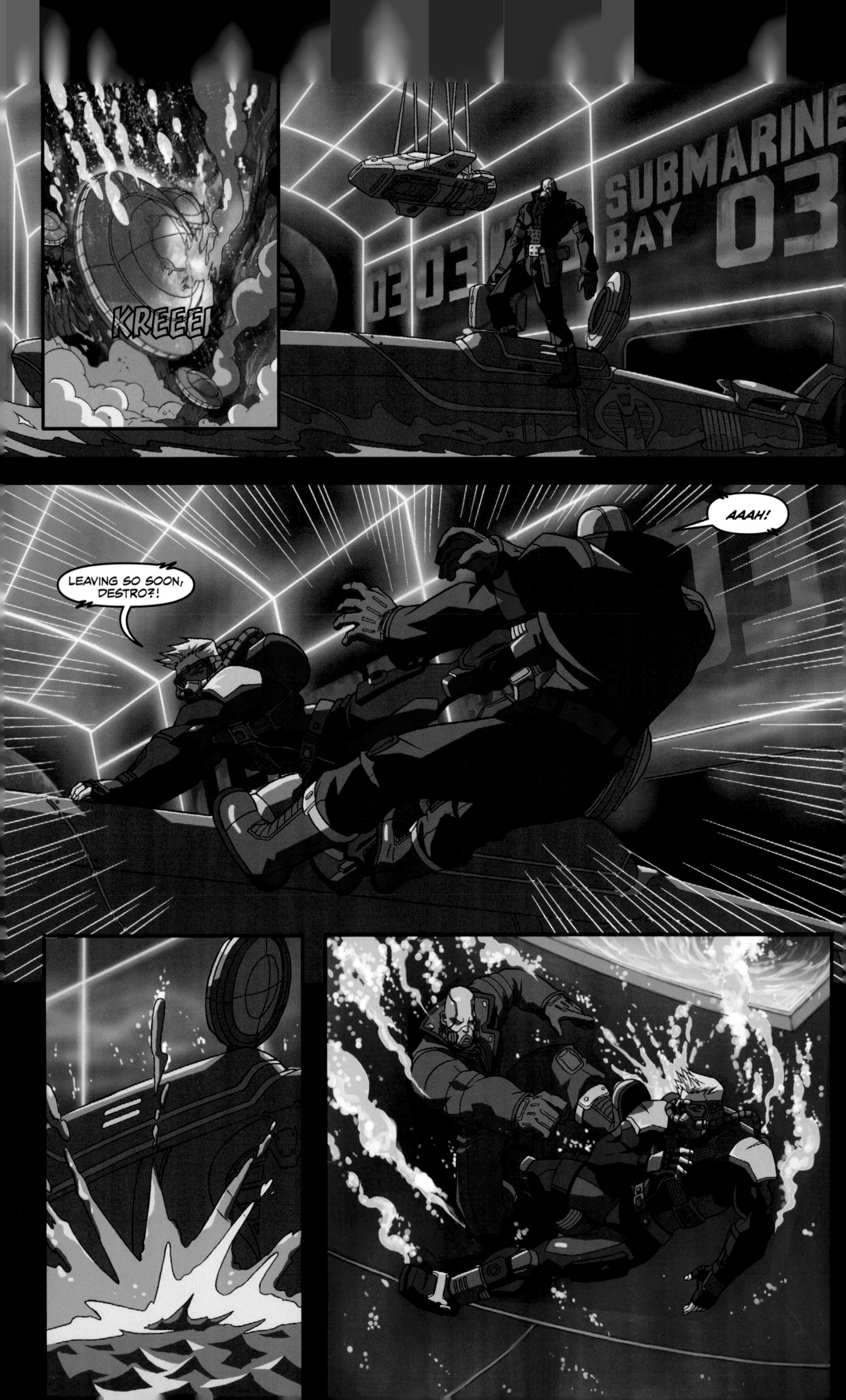
KREEEK
SUBMARINE BAY 03
0303
LEAVING SO SOON, DESTRO?!
AAAH!

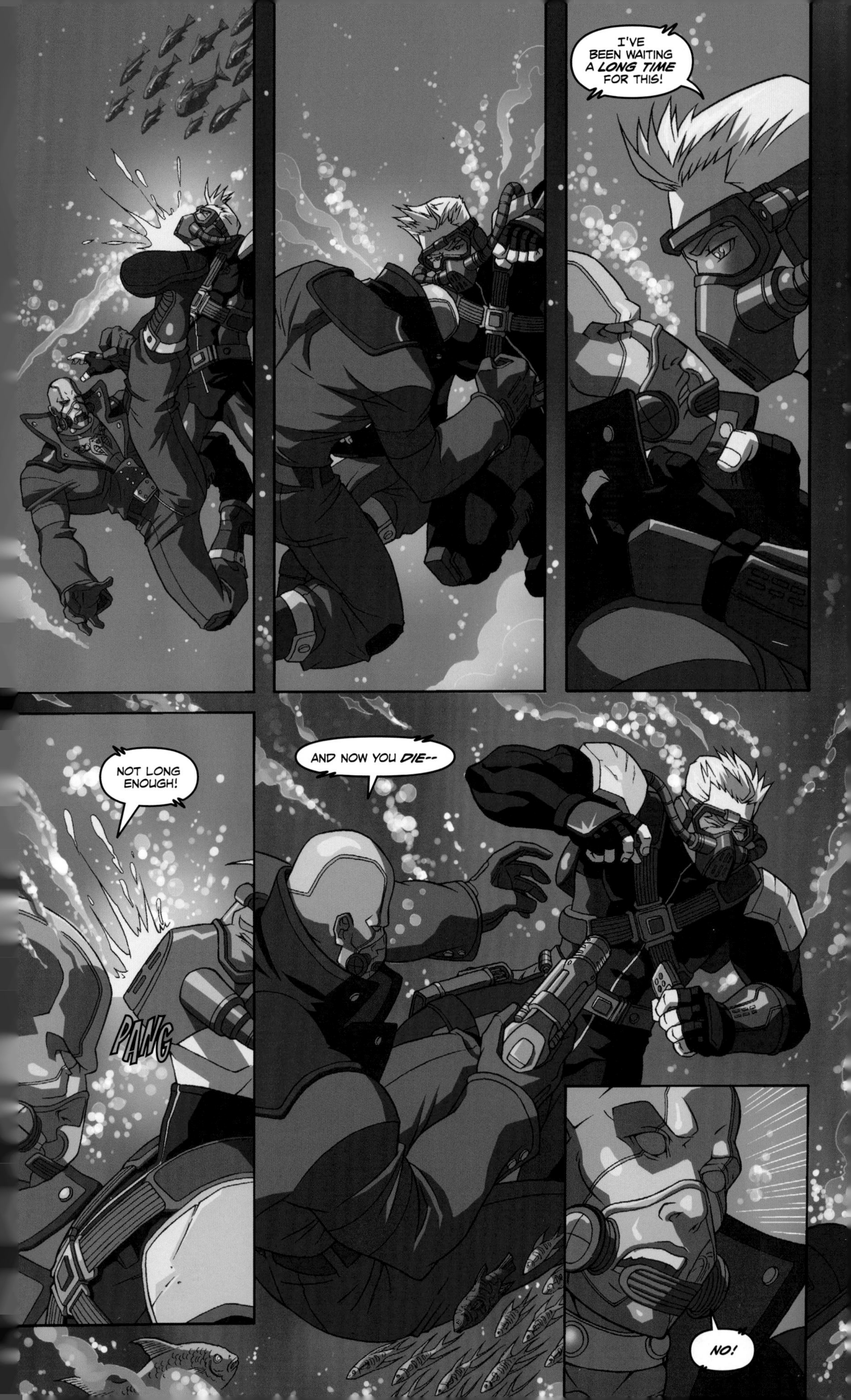
I'VE BEEN WAITING A LONG TIME FOR THIS!
NOT LONG ENOUGH!
PANG
AND NOW YOU DIE--
NO!

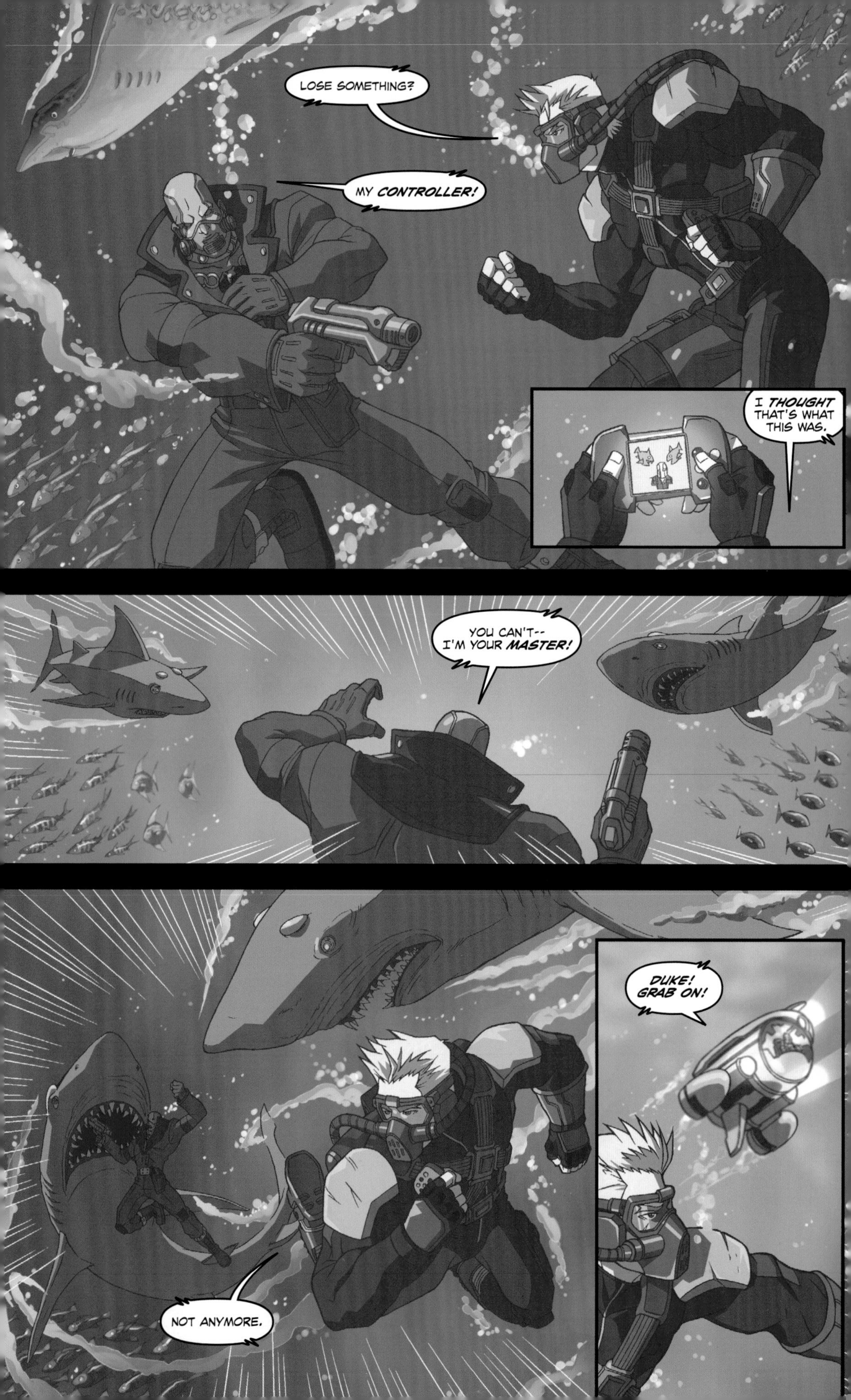
LOSE SOMETHING?
MY *CONTROLLER!*
I *THOUGHT* THAT'S WHAT THIS WAS.
YOU CAN'T-- I'M YOUR *MASTER!*
DUKE! GRAB ON!
NOT ANYMORE.

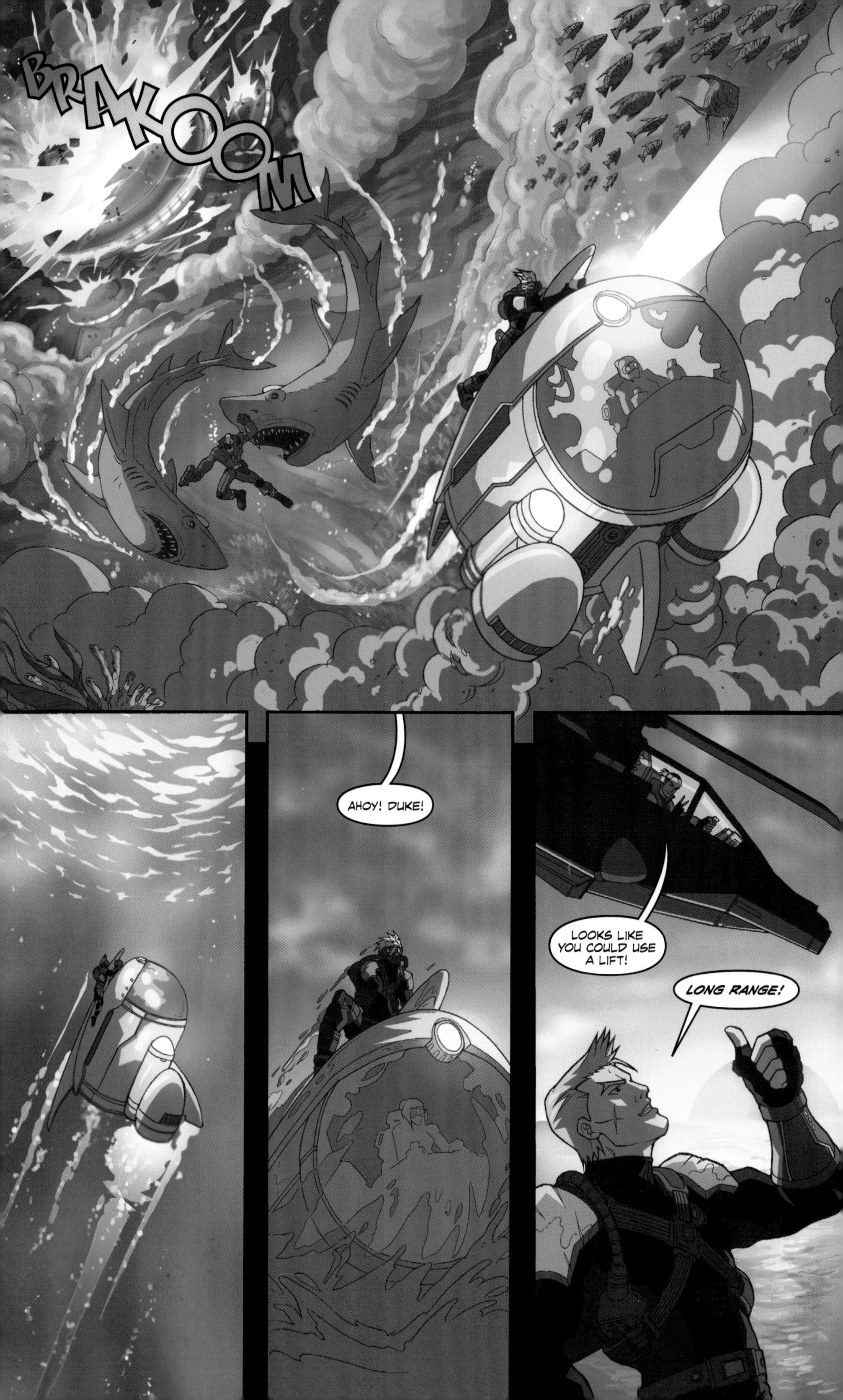
BRAKOOOM
AHOY! DUKE!
LOOKS LIKE YOU COULD USE A LIFT!
LONG RANGE!

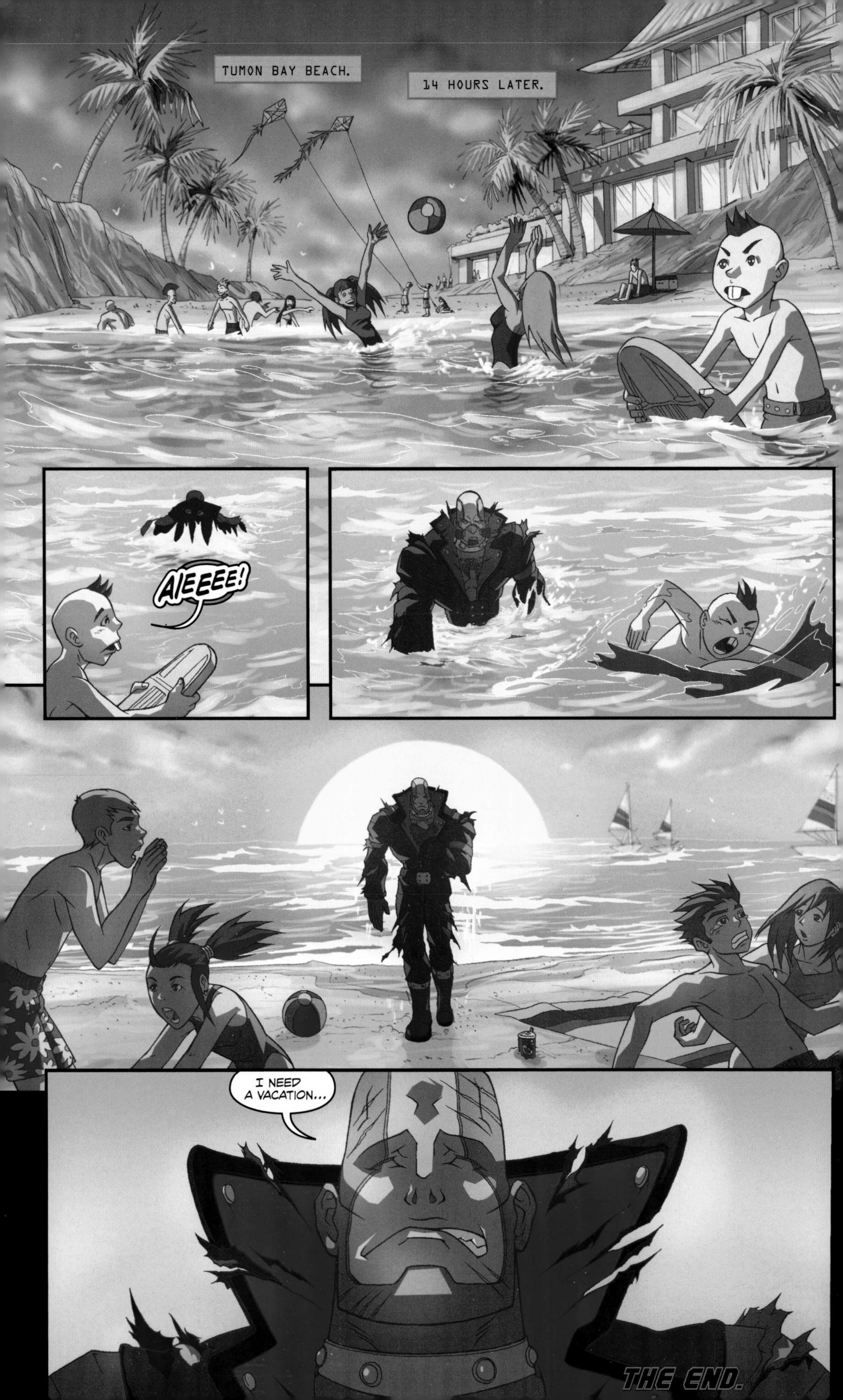
TUMON BAY BEACH.
14 HOURS LATER.
AIEEEE!
I NEED A VACATION...
THE END.